BOY + BOT

BOY + BOT

by **AME DYCKMAN**

illustrated by **DAN YACCARINO**

SCHOLASTIC INC.

For Alaric, The Boy—A.D.

For Joe Rash—D.Y.

ISBN 978-1-338-08904-2

Text copyright © 2012 by Ame Dyckman. Cover art and interior illustrations copyright © 2012 by Dan Yaccarino. All rights reserved. Published by Scholastic Inc., 557 Broadway, New York, NY 10012, by arrangement with Alfred A. Knopf, an imprint of Random House Children's Books, a division of Penguin Random House LLC. SCHOLASTIC and associated logos are trademarks and/or registered trademarks of Scholastic Inc.

12 11 10 9 8 7 6 5 4 3 2 1   16 17 18 19 20 21

Printed in the U.S.A.   40

This edition first printing, September 2016

The illustrations in this book were created using gouache on watercolor paper.

A boy was collecting pinecones in
his wagon when he met a robot.

"Hi!" said the boy. "Want to play?"
The robot blinked. "Affirmative!"

They played. They had fun.

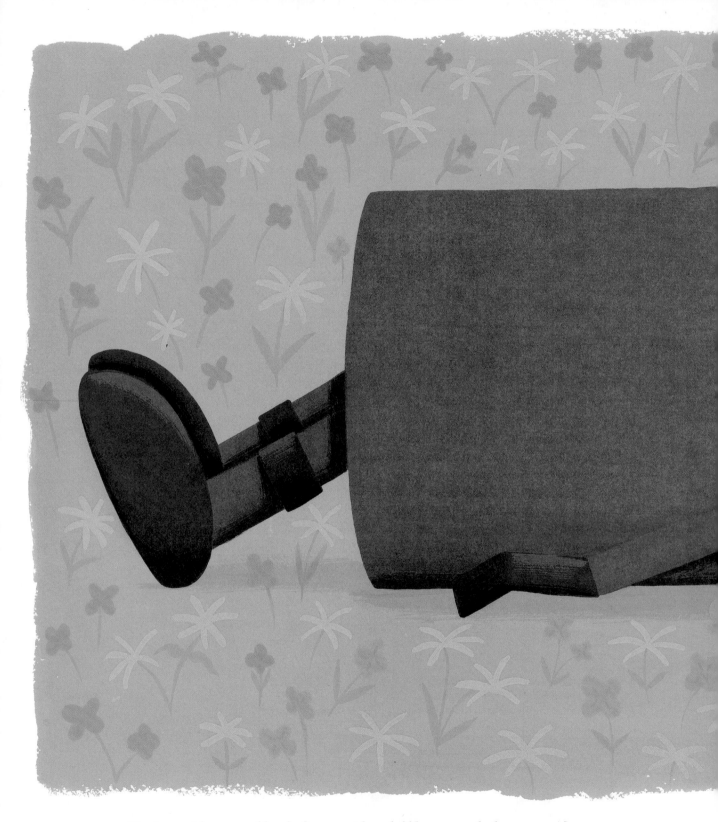

But as they rolled down the hill, a rock bumped the robot's power switch and the robot turned off. "What's wrong?" the boy asked.

The robot did not answer. "Are you sick?" the boy asked.

The robot still did not answer.

"I must help him," the boy said.

The boy fed him applesauce.

He took the robot home.

He read the robot a story.

And he tucked him in.
"Good night, Bot," the boy whispered,
and climbed into bed.

Later, the boy's parents peeked in on him.
They did not see Bot behind the door. The
door bumped Bot on his power switch.
BEEP! Bot turned on.

"What-is-wrong?" Bot asked.

The boy did not answer.

"Did-you-malfunction?" Bot asked.

The boy still did not answer. "I-must-help-him," Bot said.

He took the boy home.

Bot gave him oil.

He read the boy an instruction manual.

**He was bringing him a spare battery
when the Inventor walked in.**

"Stop!" the Inventor shouted. "That is a *boy*!"

The boy woke with a start. Then he saw Bot.
The boy smiled. "Bot! You are cured!"

Bot lit up. "Boy! You-are-fixed!"
The Inventor called Boy's parents.

Then he drove Boy home.

"Good night, Bot," Boy said.

"Good-night-Boy," Bot said. "Want-to-play-tomorrow?"

Boy nodded. "Affirmative!"

And the friends did.